Why Blue?

by Josh Tuininga

xist Publishing

First Edition. ISBN: 978-1-62395-553-3 | Published in the United States by Xist Publishing.
www.xistpublishing.com

to Klara & Hazel

Maya went for a walk
on a clear, blue day.

She sat awhile
in her favorite place.

Maya looked up at the sky
and wondered...

Why Blue?

Why not...

...HOT PINK!

Or lime green?

What stopped the sky
from being paisley?

Or plaid?!

She loved
hard questions.

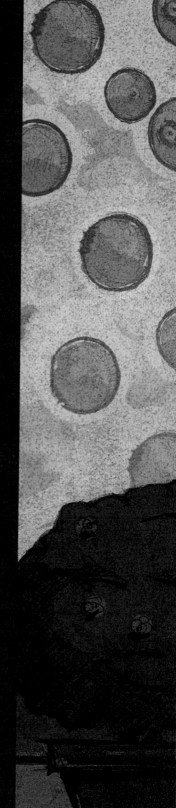

She went to visit the baker.
"Why is the sky blue?" asked Maya.

"Because," said the baker,
"I had leftover blueberries
from this morning's pancakes!"

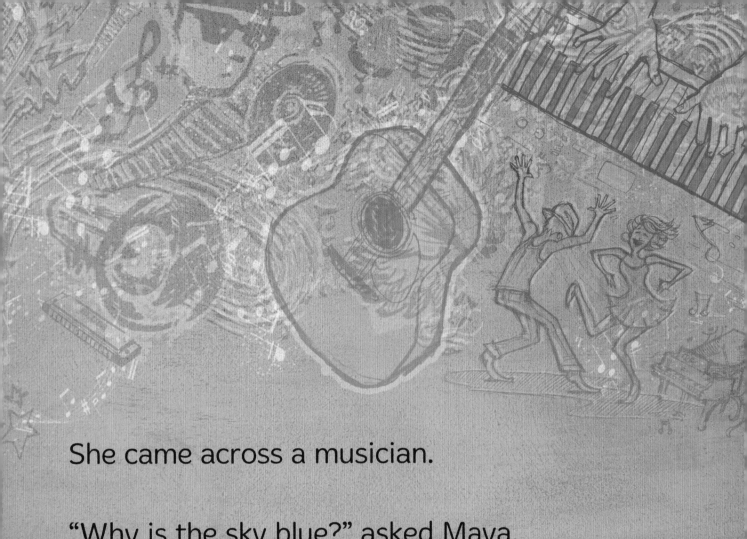

She came across a musician.

"Why is the sky blue?" asked Maya.
"Cause I'm playin' the BLUES, little gal!
The blues is the world and the world is the blues."

Across town, Maya noticed
a woman painting an old fence.

Did somebody paint
the sky blue?

Later that afternoon
she met her brother
at the high school.

"Why is the sky blue?"
asked Maya.

"It's actually quite simple. As light moves through the atmosphere, most of it passes straight through. The blue light however, gets scattered in all directions.

sunlight is made up of all the colors of the rainbow. They travel in many colors, you see, sunlight is made up of all the colors of the rainbow. This light travels in waves into

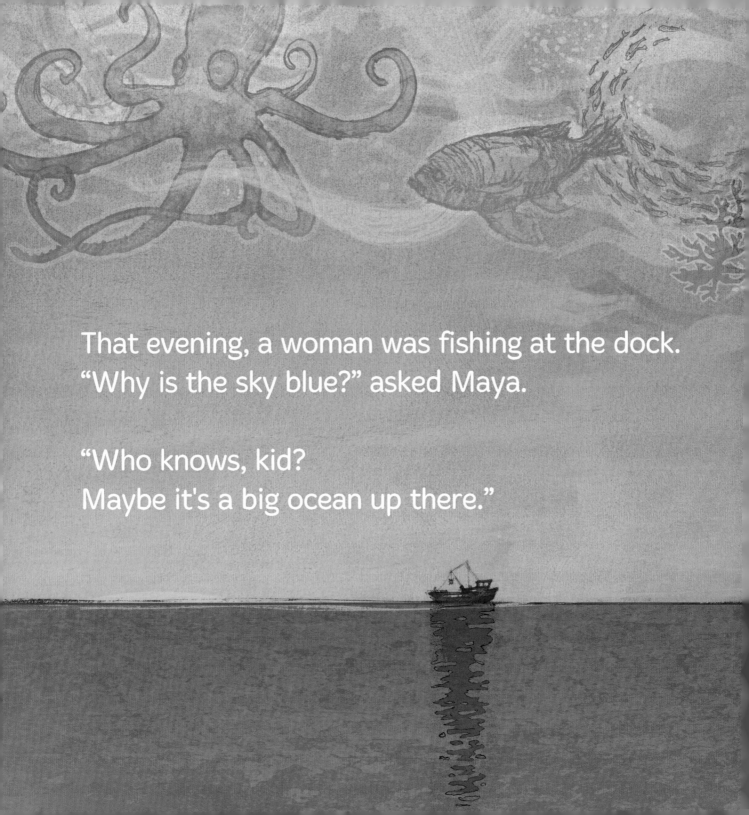

That evening, a woman was fishing at the dock.
"Why is the sky blue?" asked Maya.

"Who knows, kid?
Maybe it's a big ocean up there."

It was getting late and
Maya was still wondering.
Everyone had such a different
way of looking at things.

She needed to do some
thinking on her own.

On the way home,
Maya looked up and noticed

the sky wasn't blue at all.

And by bedtime
it had changed again.

Maya lay very still.

She looked into the
night and began to
see something.

And as she drifted off...

she made a sky
of her own.

CPSIA information can be obtained
at www.ICGtesting.com
Printed in the USA
BVXC01n0049080414
350015BV00002B/4